Penny & Jelly
Slumber Under the Stars

Written by **Maria Gianferrari**   Illustrated by **Thyra Heder**

HOUGHTON MIFFLIN HARCOURT
Boston New York

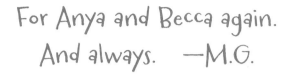

For Anya and Becca again.
And always. —M.G.

For Zoe, Alfie, and Spectacles. —T.H.

The text of this book is set in ITC Clearface.
The illustrations are watercolor, pencil, and ink.

Library of Congress Cataloging-in-Publication Data

Gianferrari, Maria.
Penny & Jelly : slumber under the stars / by Maria Gianferrari ;
illustrated by Thyra Heder.
pages cm
Summary: "Penny is thrilled to get her invitation to a slumber under the stars party, but then she realizes that no pets are allowed—and she'll have to leave her beloved dog Jelly home for the evening. With a little creative thinking, though, Penny finds a way to sleep beneath the stars and have her canine companion by her side as she does it."— Provided by publisher.
ISBN 978-0-544-28005-2
[1. Sleepovers—Fiction. 2. Dogs—Fiction.] I. Heder, Thyra, illustrator. II. Title. III. Title: Penny and Jelly. IV. Title: Slumber under the stars.
PZ7.G339028Pd 2016
[E]—dc23
2014049695

Manufactured in China | SCP 10 9 8 7 6 5 4 3 2 1
4500580999

"Hooray!" said Penny.
"Tomorrow is Sleepover Under the Stars Night, Jelly!"

To prepare, Penny and Jelly watched constellations
beam down from the bedroom ceiling.
The Big Dipper flashed.
The Pleiades, those Seven Sisters, sparkled.

The Dog Star, Sirius, shined.
The brightest in the sky, it was
Penny and Jelly's favorite.

The next day, Penny called her
friends: Kirsten, Meena, Camila,
and Riley.

They were all excited to go.

Penny made a list of all the
things she'd need:

1) sleeping bag
2) pillow
3) PJs
4) book
5) Jelly

But there was one big problem:

No pets were allowed at Sleepover
Under the Stars Night.

1) sleeping bag
2) pillow
3) PJs
4) book
5) ~~Jelly~~

"Ruff-roo-roo," barked Jelly.

"Great idea, Jelly!

If I can't bring the
real Jelly, I'll make a
pretend Jelly."

Penny colored.
She drew.
She cut.
She glued.

"Ta-da!"

It sort of looked like
Jelly, but Paper Jelly was
too hard.

No soft tongue for licking.

No fuzzy fur for petting.

No wet nose for nuzzling.

Paper Jelly was nothing like
the real Jelly.

"Ruff-roo-roo," barked Jelly,
batting a ball of yarn.

"Yes! A yarn Jelly will be perfect!"

Penny knitted.

She looped.

She braided.

She hooped.

It sort of looked like Jelly,
but Yarn Jelly was too soft.

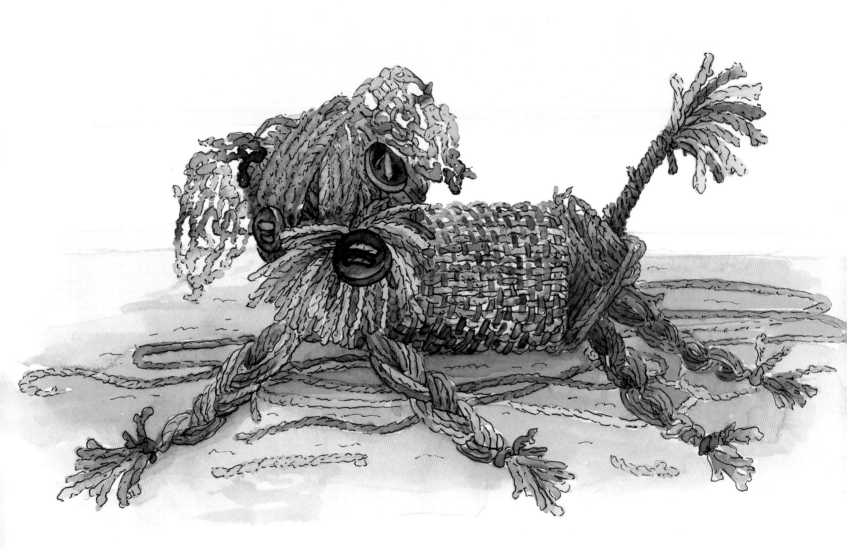

No click-clacking nails.

No wig-waggling tail.

A bit too frail.

This was not the real Jelly.

"Ruff-roooo," yawned Jelly.

"You're right, Jelly!
A piece of fleece is exactly what I need!"

Penny rolled.
She folded.

She tied.
She molded.

But Fleece Jelly was just not right.

Penny tried Jelly,

Marshmallow Jelly

Vegetable Jelly

Pipecleaner Jelly

after Jelly,

after Jelly.

Shaving Cream Jelly

Clay Jelly

Cotton Ball Jelly

~~Button Jelly~~

~~Princess Costume Jelly~~

Jelly Jelly

~~Recylable Jelly~~

But not one of them was right.

The sun was setting.
The moon was rising.

Penny imagined stars blinking
bright in the night sky.
    Penny could almost smell the
campfire burning.
    Penny could practically taste
the s'mores, sweet and sticky, on
her tongue.

Penny rolled up her sleeping bag.

She packed her pillow.

She zipped her backpack.

Her backpack was full,
but Penny felt empty
without Jelly.

Then Penny knew just what to do!

Penny and her friends ate s'mores
and slurped hot chocolate.
They sang campfire songs.
They told ghost stories.
They searched the sky for stars.

Penny slumbered under a constellation of
friends, surrounded by a galaxy of Jellys.

Even though
only one of them
was just right.

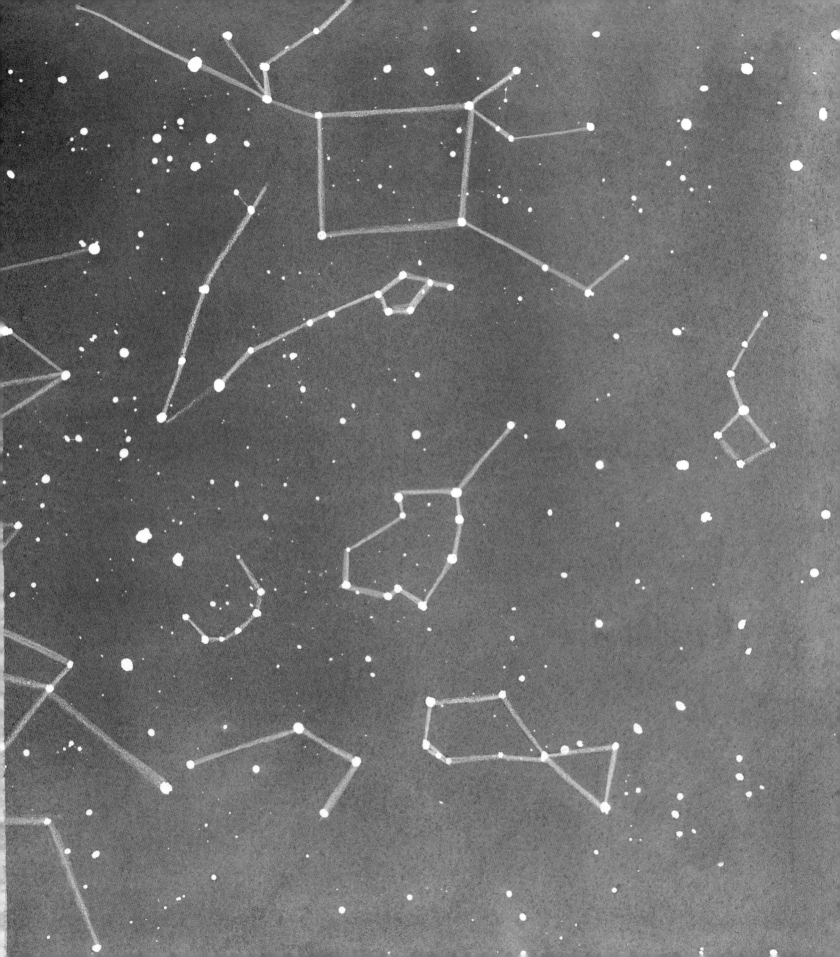